A Dozen Dozens

A Viking Math Easy-to-Read

by Harriet Ziefert
illustrated by Chris Demarest

VIKING

VIKING
Published by the Penguin Group
Penguin Putnam Inc., 375 Hudson Street, New York, New York 10014, U.S.A.
Penguin Books Ltd, 27 Wrights Lane, London W8 5TZ, England
Penguin Books Australia Ltd, Ringwood, Victoria, Australia
Penguin Books Canada Ltd, 10 Alcorn Avenue, Toronto, Ontario, Canada M4V 3B2
Penguin Books (N.Z.) Ltd, 182–190 Wairau Road, Auckland 10, New Zealand

Penguin Books Ltd, Registered Offices: Harmondsworth, Middlesex, England

First published in the United States of America by Viking, a member of Penguin Putnam Inc., 1998
Published simultaneously in Puffin Books

1 3 5 7 9 10 8 6 4 2

LIBRARY OF CONGRESS CATALOGING-IN-PUBLICATION DATA
Ziefert, Harriet.
A dozen dozens / by Harriet Ziefert ; pictures by Chris L. Demarest.
p. cm.
Summary : Illustrations and rhyming text present dozens—or half-
dozens—of pigs, tulips, apples, eggs, socks, babies, and more.
Includes related activities.
ISBN 0-670-87789-1 (hc). — ISBN 0-14-038819-2 (pbk. : alk. paper)
[1. Twelve (The number)—Fiction. 2. Stories in rhyme.]
I. Demarest, Chris L., ill. II. Title.
PZ8.3.Z47Do 1998 [E]—dc21 97-15353 CIP AC

Printed in U.S.A.
Set in Bookman

Reading level 2.3

A Dozen Dozens

What is a dozen?

A dozen is a group of twelve,
Twelve things large or small.
Here are twelve fat piglets—
Count them, one and all.

What is a half dozen?

Let's count up half a dozen.
That's six of anything:
Six tulips or six roses—
They smell just like spring.

A dozen eggs are in the barn.
Six of them have cracks.
Two chicks are peeking out,
Their shells still on their backs.

I love a yummy apple pie.
My sister Sue likes peach.
All together we have twelve—
Or half a dozen each.

Half a dozen apples,
Half a dozen more.
I've got a dozen apples
Inside my desk drawer.

If I had a dozen feet,
I'd need six pairs of socks.
I'd fold them all up neatly
In a big purple box.

My father ate two slices.
My mother wanted three.
My sister wanted only one,
Leaving six for me!

Twelve big goldfish
Swimming in a school.
Guess how many goldfish
Will be left in the pool?

Dog has eleven cousins.
He's one of a dozen.
Do you know anybody
With so many cousins?

Mary has quadruplets.
Her brother Tom has twins.
That's half a dozen babies
With banana on their chins.

These two sets of triplets
Belong to Suzy Jane.
That's half a dozen kids
Walking in the rain.

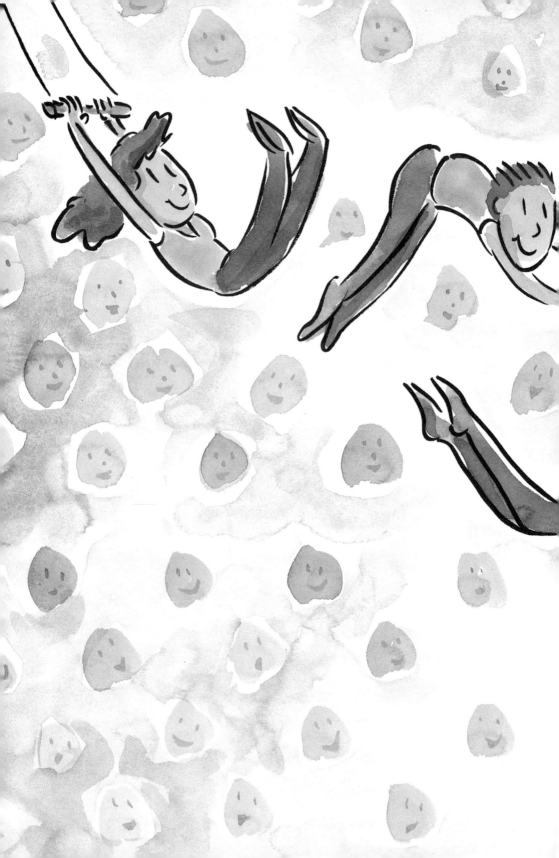

Half a dozen acrobats,
Twelve legs in the air . . .

Another half a dozen,
Balanced on a chair!

FAMILY MATH FUN

- In your house, are there a dozen

Chairs?	Windows?	Pots?
Spoons?	Steps?	Pans?
Glasses?	Lamps?	Pictures?

Count and find out. Are there exactly one dozen, more than one dozen, or less than one dozen?

- Do you know the names of a dozen different kinds of dinosaurs? Make a list of the ones you know, then ask a grown-up to help you until your list has twelve kinds. You can also try to list a dozen kinds of dogs, bugs, or birds.

- Write a story about a dozen bugs, or a dozen dogs, or a dozen cats, or a dozen dinosaurs. Make pictures to go with the words.

- Do you have a dozen of anything? What? If you don't, perhaps you would like to collect a dozen rocks, or a dozen stamps, or a dozen acorns, or a dozen new pennies, or a dozen marbles.

- Look in the telephone book. Are there a dozen families with the same last name as yours? More than a dozen? Less than a dozen?